Date Due

MAR 1 1 1991			
DEC 1 4 1995			

The Spooky Eerie Night Noise

by **Mona Rabun Reeves**
illustrated by **Paul Yalowitz**

Bradbury Press   New York

Bradbury Press
An Affiliate of Macmillan, Inc.
866 Third Avenue, New York, NY 10022
Collier Macmillan Canada, Inc.
Printed and bound by South China Printing Company, Hong Kong
First American Edition
10 9 8 7 6 5 4 3 2 1

The text of this book is set in Fenice.
The illustrations are rendered in colored pencil, reproduced in full color.
Book design by Julie Quan

LIBRARY OF CONGRESS CATALOGING-IN-PUBLICATION DATA
Reeves, Mona R.
   The spooky eerie night noise.
   Summary: Jenny hears something outside and imagines all kinds of
spooky explanations until she and her parents decide to investigate.
   [1. Fear—Fiction. 2. Night—Fiction. 3. Stories in rhyme]
I. Yalowitz, Paul, ill. II. Title. PZ8.3.R263Sp 1989 [E] 89-447
ISBN 0-02-775732-3

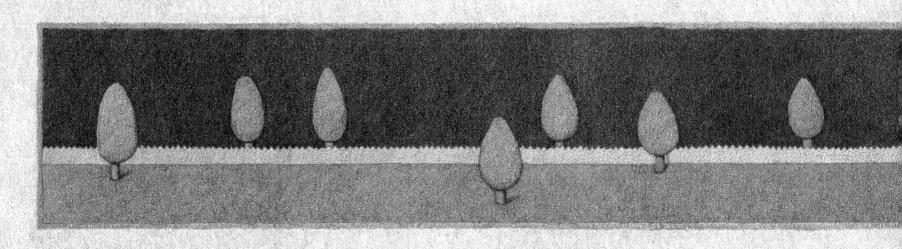

In loving memory of my parents, Katherine and Dick Rabun,
who always understood...
—M.R.R.

Dedicated to my mother and father and the bathroom light
that they always left on at night
—P.Y.

A spooky noise from our backyard!
My heart starts thumping,
bumping hard.
It's dark outside.

It's night.

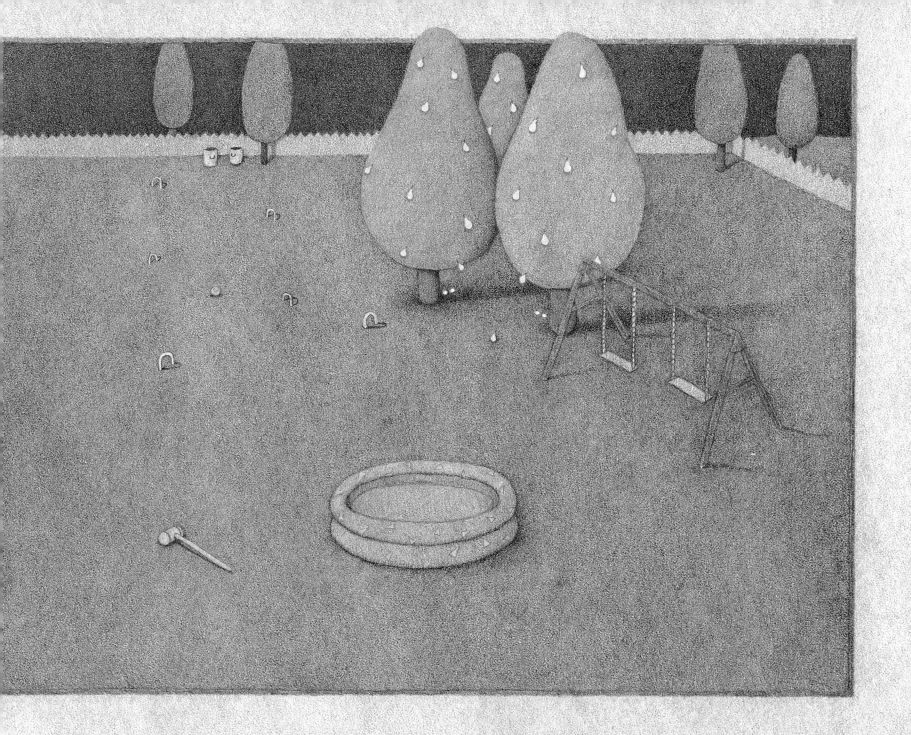

I find it hard to catch my breath. That scritchy noise scares me to death.
I'm holding Barney tight.

What could it be? A monster's feet? A ghostly figure in a sheet?
My mind begins to race.

A wicked witch?
A criminal?
A huge ferocious animal?
A ship
from outer space?

A beast like I have never seen,
with purple hair
and horns of green?

A lion with a fuzzy mane?

An eerie ghoul? A dinosaur?
The nightmare from
my dresser drawer?
A spook
with a clanking chain?

A creepy, crawly giant snake? A jittery old sprite?
A terrifying caravan of dreadful things

that bite?

That sound again! . . . A crocodile?

A vampire with an evil smile?

My mom and dad are sitting there,
reading in their easy chairs.
I croak, "Did you hear that?"

Dad says, "Could be the cat."

I see a tiger in my mind—
the angry, snarly,
hungry kind.
My throat is feeling tight.
I try to keep from *shivering*,
to stop my knees from
quivering.
I hope my dad is right.

But no!

Here is the cat inside!
I think of places I can hide
when creatures
smash the door.

I hear the gremlins *prowling* and

I hear the werewolves *howling* and

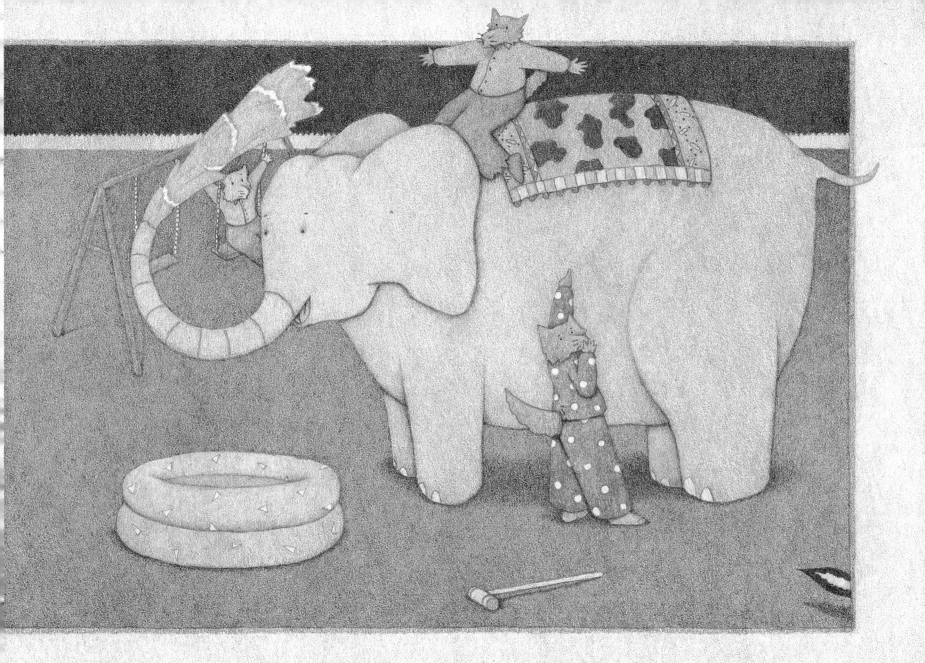

I hear the elephants *roar!*

I feel the goose bumps on my skin.
I hear that spooky sound
again!

Whatever could it be?

My voice is shaky as I say,
"I wish that noise would go away."
My mom looks up at me.
"What noise?" she says. "I didn't hear."
My dad asks,
"What's wrong, Jenny dear?"
I smile to show my grit.

I whisper, "Something's out in back. It may be bad. It could attack.
I'm scared . . . a little bit."

"We'll check it out. I'll get a light." My mom says, "It will be all right."
I'm feeling braver now.

We're peering out into the back.
The flashlight beam
cuts through the black.
My dad says, "Holy cow!"

Four eyes reflect back in the light
like glowing embers in the night
around the pear-tree trunks.
We see the white stripes
down their backs.
We laugh,
and leave them to their snacks,

that pair of **Hungry Skunks!**